To Jack

Northamptonshire Libraries & Information Service	
80 002 597 623	
Peters	02-Feb-06
CF	£5.99

BABY BEAR'S CHRISTMAS KISS
A RED FOX BOOK 0 099 43963 8

First published in Great Britain by The Bodley Head,
an imprint of Random House Children's Books

The Bodley Head edition published 2004
Red Fox edition published 2005

1 3 5 7 9 10 8 6 4 2

Copyright © John Prater, 2004

The right of John Prater to be identified as the author and
illustrator of this work has been asserted in accordance
with the Copyright, Designs and Patents Act 1988.

All rights reserved. No part of this publication may be reproduced, stored in a retrieval system,
or transmitted in any form or by any means, electronic, mechanical, photocopying,
recording or otherwise, without the prior permission of the publishers.

Red Fox Books are published by Random House Children's Books,
61–63 Uxbridge Road, London W5 5SA,
a division of The Random House Group Ltd,
in Australia by Random House Australia (Pty) Ltd,
20 Alfred Street, Milsons Point, Sydney, NSW 2061, Australia,
in New Zealand by Random House New Zealand Ltd,
18 Poland Road, Glenfield, Auckland 10, New Zealand,
and in South Africa by Random House (Pty) Ltd,
Endulini, 5A Jubilee Road, Parktown 2193, South Africa

THE RANDOM HOUSE GROUP Limited Reg. No. 954009
www.kidsatrandomhouse.co.uk

A CIP catalogue record for this book is available from the British Library.

Printed in Singapore

80 002 597 623

Baby Bear's Christmas Kiss

Baby Bear's Christmas Kiss

JOHN PRATER

RED FOX

It was Christmas Day!
The whole family were visiting Baby Bear and
Grandbear. That's Granny Bear, Uncle Bear,
Auntie Bear and four Cousin Bears.
The grown-ups warmed up by the fire,
while the little ones put their presents
under the tree. But they didn't seem
to be able to leave them alone.

Every present was shaken . . .

. . . prodded

. . . and sniffed.

Grandbear had an idea.
"You can open just one
present each, now!"

All the cousins ripped open their presents.

"Wow!" said Baby Bear. "What is it?"
"It's a toboggan," said Grandbear.
"What's a 'boggan?"
asked Baby Bear.
"I'll show you,"
said Uncle Bear.
"Come outside with me."

"Up the hill
we go!"
said Uncle Bear.

"Now watch closely,"
said Uncle Bear.
"First, you . . ."

"Hey!" cried Uncle Bear. "Wait! . . ."

Faster and *faster*
went Uncle Bear . . .

. . . until he met up with a snowbear!

"That was really funny," said Baby Bear.
"Can we have a go, now?"

Up the hill
they went again . . .

. . . and down they came!

Again and again until Uncle Bear said . . .

"Oooh, I can smell yummy cooking.
It's time to go inside."

Grandbear met them at the door.
"Hello, snowbears! You're just
in time for Christmas dinner."

What a feast!

After dinner, the grown-ups were so
full they could hardly move.
The little ones played hide-and-seek.

It didn't take Baby Bear long to
find Big Cousin Bear hiding under
the tree. "This is my present to
Mum and Dad," said Big Cousin
Bear. "What are you giving
Grandbear?"

"I haven't got a
present for Grandbear!"
said Baby Bear.
"Never mind,"
said Big Cousin Bear.
"It's your turn to
hide now!"

While the others covered their eyes, and counted to ten, Baby Bear crept out of the room, through the kitchen, and into the garden.

But Baby Bear wasn't hiding. Baby Bear was going to find a present for Grandbear.

Grandbear likes snow, thought Baby Bear.
And stars. Something glistened and caught
Baby Bear's eye . . .

Baby Bear looked closer.
"Snowberries!"
said Baby Bear.
"All twinkly like
the star on the
Christmas
tree!"

Baby Bear picked
some berries, then
started to make
something out
of snow.

When it was
finished,
Baby Bear
hurried
back inside.

"Found you!"
called Cousin Bear.
"Come on, we're opening
the presents now."

Everyone was very excited!

"Happy Christmas, Grandbear!" said Baby Bear. "I brought you a snowberry snowbear!"

"Mistletoe!" said Grandbear. "That deserves a special Christmas kiss! I'll put your lovely present somewhere where it won't melt."

All the grown-ups asked

if they could have a

Christmas kiss too.

The little ones weren't too sure, though.

Happy Christmas, Baby Bear!
Happy Christmas, everyone!

Other Baby Bear books to share:

The Bear Went Over the Mountain

JOHN PRATER

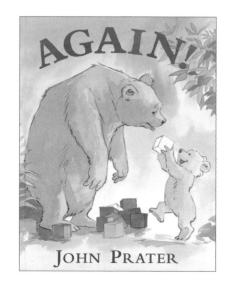

AGAIN!

JOHN PRATER

JOHN PRATER

Oh Where, Oh Where?

Is It Christmas?

JOHN PRATER

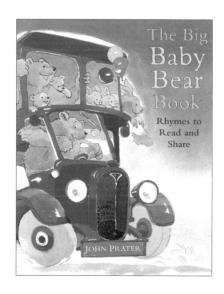

The Big BABY BEAR Book

Rhymes to Read and Share

JOHN PRATER

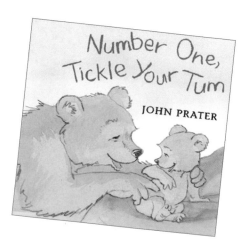

Number One, Tickle Your Tum

JOHN PRATER

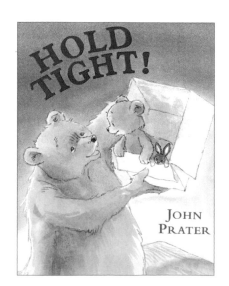

HOLD TIGHT!

JOHN PRATER

JOHN PRATER

Walking Round the Garden